Mama

Mama

Lee Bennett Hopkins

Boyds Mills Press

Published by Caroline House
Boyds Mills Press, Inc.
A Highlights Company
815 Church Street
Honesdale, Pennsylvania 18431
Printed in the United States of America

Publisher Cataloging-in-Publication Data
Hopkins, Lee Bennett.
Mama / by Lee Bennett Hopkins.
[80]p. ;   cm.
Originally published : New York: Knopf, 1977.
Summary: A mother struggles to feed, clothe, and protect her two sons
using whatever resources she can muster, including stealing.
ISBN 1-56397-813-X
1. Mothers and sons—Fiction—Juvenile literature. 2.Stealing—
Fiction—Juvenile literature. [1. Mothers and sons—Fiction.
2. Stealing—Fiction.] I. Title.
813.54 [F]—dc21   1999   AC   CIP

Library of Congress Catalog Card Number 99-60224

First edition, 2000
The text of this book is set in 12-point Garamond.

10 9 8 7 6 5 4 3 2 1

To
Pat who saw . . .
Misha who saw it through . . .
AND FOR . . .
my own Mama

—L. B. H.

One

*"You know your Mama never likes to say
anything bad about people, but ..."*

"DID YOU EVER THINK WE'D MAKE IT, MAMA?" I asked,
plopping down on the couch, too tired to move another muscle.

"It was a lot of work!" Mama answered. "More work than your
Mama imagined it would be, but I knew we could do it. We
worked hard today, all three of us did, but moving from the
seventh floor to the third in the same apartment building isn't
half as hard as moving *out* of the building. We were lucky this
apartment was empty, and that the super kept us in mind. We
were luckier still that I could get a day off from the department
store."

Mama went on and on.

"Another good thing about this place, son, is that we know who lived here before we took it. Donna and Jay were a nice, clean couple—for young people. That girl was brought up right: brought up to keep a clean house."

I started to undo one of the boxes, one ear tuned in to Mama's endless conversation, the other ear tuned in to my own thoughts about the new place.

The apartment was clean, as Mama said, but it was so crowded. Our old apartment on the seventh floor had five and a half large rooms. But Mama couldn't afford the rent any longer. This one has four small rooms: a tiny kitchen, a living room, a bedroom that my little brother and I will share, and Mama's room. The bathroom is hardly big enough to hold the tub. I guess that's why they don't count it as a room.

Since Mama never throws anything away—ever—everything that was in the five-and-a-half-room apartment is squeezed into this one. The living room looks like a department store. Tables are next to tables, chairs next to chairs. Every time you move, you bump into something. There isn't even a crack between anything. Lamps are everywhere.

There is at least one lamp on every table; some tables have two or three lamps. There are hanging lamps, too—hanging over the lamps standing on the tables! We probably have a fortune just in light bulbs. I'm sure that if one more lamp is plugged into one more socket, the whole apartment house is going to explode into a million bits.

Then there are Mama's knickknacks—things like salt and pepper lovebirds, a set of china figurines dressed in peasant costumes, and a merry-go-round that plays a song called "The Impossible Dream." Mama likes that best. Things like these are all over the tables and windowsills. Some are even on the kitchen counter.

Looking around, I also realized how much plastic we have. Mama loves things made out of plastic—plastic dishes, plastic glasses, plastic tables, plastic lamps, plastic slipcovers covering the couch and chairs—even plastic plants.

"Real plants are for people who sit home all day long and do nothing, like your Great-aunt Bertha up in Yonkers," Mama said. "When you're a hard-working woman, like your Mama, you don't have the time to fool around, puttering with dirt and pots and water. Plastic plants are easier to care for. All you have to do is dust them off once in a while, and when they get too much dust and dirt on them, you can just fling them out and buy new ones. They're also cheaper than real ones, and you don't ever have to water them. Never. But I like to keep some of those plastic watering cans near them," Mama added with a laugh, "'cause that way some people think they're real."

As usual, Mama wasn't ready to leave Great-aunt Bertha alone just yet, and on she went.

"Your Great-aunt Bertha raises some kind of real violets that come from Africa. I don't know why that woman can't be happy with American violets. Plastic is American, and I'd only have plastic violets in my house—*American* plastic violets. Let the Africans take care of their own violets!

"You know your Mama never likes to say anything bad about people, especially a blood-relative, but your Great-aunt Bertha never did a day's work in her life. If she had to she'd die. She's content being a housewife and letting your poor old Great-uncle Albert go out day after day to make a living. Any woman who sits around all day long puttering with foreign violets between TV shows should be ashamed of the air she breathes in and out. She's not like your Mama."

"Yes, Mama," I replied, at the same time thinking, who is? There's no one like my Mama—no one anywhere!

"That woman should be ashamed of the air she breathes in and out," she repeated.

"So why are we going up to visit her next Sunday?" I asked, expecting Mama to avoid answering me.

"We haven't seen her in a long time, and she keeps asking us up. Your Mama just couldn't put her off any longer. I think she's still upset about your daddy and me, and now that we've moved, I think she's wondering how we'll get along. That woman sure can be a busybody. But we're only going up for lunch. We won't stay a minute more than we have to—just long enough to show her that the three of us are doing fine. Even though Great-aunt Bertha is not one of my favorite people to visit, she is a blood-relative. I did promise her that we'd come up one day, and next Sunday is that one day."

Mama stopped and picked up the last box. "Let's not talk about Great-aunt Bertha anymore for now. Let's talk about good things—all the good things Mama is going to do for you and your little brother. Won't that train ride up to Yonkers be lots of fun, especially for your little brother? He's never been on a train that runs *above* the ground. All he knows is the subway. The train ride will be like a treat."

"I hope Great-aunt Bertha doesn't make you feel bad like she usually does," I said.

"Don't you worry about your Mama, son. Your Mama can hold her own. That woman gives advice like she was some famous TV personality. Without TV, I don't think your Great-aunt Bertha would have a thought of her own. Your Mama has one thing in this world that your Great-aunt Bertha never had or ever will have. Mama's got you and your little brother. Nothing will ever be more important to me than the two of you. Now why don't we stop talking about Great-aunt Bertha? There's no need to think about an old fussbudget the likes of her."

"O.K., Mama," I said, but I couldn't help thinking about Great-aunt Bertha. Every time we see her she gives Mama lectures about everything. Every sentence starts something like: "The boys should do this," or "The boys shouldn't do that," or "The boys need this," or "The boys don't need that," or "You should try not to work so hard."

Suddenly Mama was back on one of her favorite subjects again —cleanliness. And I was supposed to be paying attention.

"Yes, we sure were lucky we didn't have to move into someone else's filth. Why, the oven and refrigerator are as clean as clean could be. Mama can always tell people's characters by their refrigerators and ovens. Good people keep their kitchens clean and fresh."

"Why did Donna and Jay move?" I asked.

"They needed a bigger place. Donna is in the family way."

"I didn't know she was pregnant," I said.

"Where did you hear that word? 'In the family way' sounds more polite than the word you used. Mama would rather we didn't talk about such things at all. Not yet. You have a lot of time before you start thinking about and using such words."

"Aw, Mama, I know all about having babies."

"Your Mama doesn't want to know all the things you know. You kids today know too much! When I was your age, I didn't know such things and wouldn't have dared to use such a word in front of *my* Mama, may she rest in peace. I didn't know about having babies until I got married and had you.

"Why don't you go wash up, put on your pajamas, and get ready for bed?" Mama said, putting an end to the subject. "But try to be quiet so you don't wake your little brother up."

"I'll be quiet, Mama. I'll be right back."

"If you have to make, wash your hands after," Mama added. "There's a fresh bar of soap and clean towel in there. Wash your hands every time after you go to the bathroom. Clean hands give you a clean heart."

"Yes, Mama," I said, stumbling through the maze of furniture trying to get to the bathroom.

The bathroom was as crowded as all the other rooms. It was small enough to begin with when it was empty, but now there is hardly a space to turn around in.

Every bit of wall space is taken up with shelves. Each shelf is packed with things—bottle after bottle of Mama's perfumes, towels, and washcloths galore; even the medicine chest bursts with stuff—stuff that we never used when we lived upstairs and probably will never use here. Thank goodness my little brother is big enough to bathe himself. Two people could never get into this room at the same time.

When I finished washing up and walked back into the living room, Mama was sound asleep, sitting up in the chair.

"Mama," I whispered gently, shaking her arm so I wouldn't startle her. "Mama, it's time to go to bed now."

Mama looked very tired.

"What time is it?" she asked groggily.

"It's after ten. Let me help you to your room, Mama."

"Mama can make it by herself," she said, getting up. "You get to bed, too. You worked hard this week, and I'm proud of that. Mama's proud of *both* of you."

"I didn't mind the move, Mama. Really I didn't."

"That's because you're a fine boy. You're strong—just like your Mama. We come from good stock."

Looking around the room, Mama paused for a minute and said,

"Everything looks so pretty in this place. We have a new house now, and we'll have a new life together here. Turn off the lights now and get to bed. I'm going to kiss your little brother good night. The poor kid's knocked out from all this moving. Try not to wake him up.

"Good night, son," Mama whispered, giving me a hug and kissing me on the top of my head. "Mama loves you. Sleep tight and don't let the bedbugs bite."

"Good night, Mama. I love you, too, and I won't."

"You won't what?"

"Let the bedbugs bite," I teased.

Mama laughed. She always says that to my little brother and me before we go to bed. Mama says funny things sometimes.

Two

"Your Mama's always right—most of the time."

"**H**OW FAR IS IT TO YUNKERS?" my little brother asked Mama.

"YONK-ers," Mama said. "Say YONK. YONK-ers!"

"How far is it to YONK-ers?" repeated my little brother.

"You've been there before," I said. "When you were a baby."

"I don't remember things when I was a baby. I only remember now things," he answered.

"Anybody want another piece of toast?" asked Mama.

"I'll have another piece please, Mama," I said.

"You'll have another piece when you finish that one."

"I did finish it," I said.

"What about the crust? Bread's not to be wasted—not at all. Bread is God's food. Eat your crust. It'll give you curly hair."

"I don't want curly hair," I answered.

"Eat it anyway," Mama commanded. "Do what your Mama says. There's a lot of backtalk in this kitchen this morning. If you'd eat that crust, your mouth wouldn't have room for backtalk."

"O.K. I'll eat the stupid crust."

Mama gave me a look that told me I shouldn't have said "stupid crust." Sometimes, one of Mama's looks says more than a million words.

Getting up from the table, Mama asked my little brother, "Do you want a piece, too?"

"I hate toast," my little brother grumbled.

"It's not nice to hate," Mama said. "This world has enough hate in it. My boys love. Mama hates hate! Your mind gets sick if you hate too much. You read and remember that sign up there," she said, pointing to the painted sign above the kitchen doorway.

"I can't read," my little brother said. "You know I can't read yet."

"You can read *that* sign," Mama told him. "It says *Love One Another*. Even if you can't read it, remember it. *Love One Another*. Once you remember it, you'll know how to read it. That's what reading is all about. Remembering words. That sign cost Mama four dollars, so you read and remember what it says. Always!"

"What does loving one another have to do with toast?" my little brother asked. "I love you, Mama, but I hate toast. Toast isn't one another, is it?"

"I think it's time you minded that tiny tongue of yours, son, that's what your Mama thinks. You do what I say, you hear?"

"All I do is get yelled at," my little brother complained, playing with his bowl of Froot Loops. "Nobody answers me. Nobody."

"What do you want answered, son?" Mama asked.

"All I want to know is how far away Yunkers is?"

"YONK-ers," Mama said. "YONK."

"Yunkers, Yenkers, Yinkers, Yankers," babbled my little brother.

"YONK-ers," repeated Mama, "is about a half-hour from Grand Central Terminal. Your Great-aunt Bertha will pick us up at the train station. Her house is only a few minutes from the train station. If we don't get a move on, we'll miss the train.

"While you're finishing your toast," she said directly to me, "crust and all—I'll get your little brother ready. We have to look extra nice for your Great-aunt Bertha. Otherwise she'll have something to say. Mama's not in the mood to hear her complaints all day long. That woman can find something to complain about even when there's *nothing* to complain about. When you finish your breakfast, start getting ready."

"Can I bring my Old Maids with me?" my little brother asked.

"You won't have time to play Old Maids today. We're not staying there that long. We're only going up for lunch, and then we're coming right back home."

"Shucks!" my little brother said. "I love to play Old Maids."

"Mama doesn't have the time now to argue with you. You just do what I say. When we get home tonight, Mama will play a game of Old Maids with you before you go to bed. Now get into the bedroom and let's pick out your nicest suit. We have to look extra nice for your Great-aunt Bertha. Extra, extra nice."

"This place is big," my little brother said, looking wildly around Grand Central Terminal.

"It's crowded, too," I added. "I never saw so many people dashing around."

"Just hold close together," Mama said. "Hold close together so no one gets lost. We have to go downstairs to the lower level for the train."

"There it is," I said, spotting the sign that read: TO LOWER LEVEL TRAINS.

"Good," said Mama. "Let's go."

We walked down a narrow stairway that led to another narrow stairway. When we reached the lower level, Mama said, "I want the two of you to stand right here in front of this newsstand while I go over there to the ticket booth to get a ticket for the train. Don't either of you move! Just stand right there. Mama will only be a minute. Just a minute."

"Why do we have to wait *here?* Can't we go to the ticket booth with you?" my little brother asked.

"Do what you're told to do, and don't move. Mama will only be a minute. Just a minute," she said, as she dashed across the lobby, always looking back at us, on her way to the ticket booth.

It seemed that she no sooner left than she was back again. She was gone less than a minute. We wouldn't have had time to move even if we'd wanted to.

"You were fast," my little brother told Mama who was all out of breath. "Can I hold my ticket?"

"You don't need a ticket," Mama told him. "Only grown-ups need tickets."

"How come?" I asked.

"Mama's getting just a lit-tle tired of all these questions. You know your Mama doesn't like questions—only answers."

"But —" I started.

"But, but, but. No more questions and no more "buts" or there are going to be two boys in this terminal who are going to get their real butts hit on a little bit! Let's go now. We have to find

Track 116. The man at the ticket window said our train is near ready for boarding.

"Sir?" Mama asked the man behind the newsstand. "Can you please tell me where Track 116 is?"

"Questions! Questions! Questions!" the man angrily replied. "All I do is answer questions all day long. Where's this? Where's that? This is a newsstand, lady, not an information center."

The man sounded like Mama. He didn't like questions either!

"Well, pardon me," Mama said with a huff. "I did say *please,* you know. I don't come here often, and I'm not sure where things are. You needn't be so impolite to people. If people were nicer to one another, *sir*, this world wouldn't be so troubled. I don't think you're setting a good example talking to me like that in front of my two young sons. You're not setting a good example at all. Not at all."

"Whoa!" the man exclaimed. "The last thing I need today is a mother."

"And what do you mean by that?" Mama asked.

"Nothing, lady. Forget it! I only run this newsstand. I don't run Grand Central Terminal."

"I can appreciate that," Mama said, "and I'd appreciate it more if you would tell me now where Track 116 is."

"It's over there," the man said, pointing to a sign across the lobby floor.

"Thank you," said Mama. "If you told me that when I asked you, you wouldn't have wasted your time and you wouldn't have gotten your feathers ruffled!

"Come along boys and hold close together. We have to go across the lobby like this *gentleman* told us to.

"Have a good day, *sir*," Mama added, looking straight into the man's eyes with one of her if-looks-could-kill-you looks.

As we walked to Track 116, Mama said to me, "As soon as we get on the train, Mama wants you to take your little brother right into the toilet. Right into the toilet!"

"I don't have to make," my little brother said.

"I didn't say you did. Just be quiet and listen to your Mama. When we get on the train," she started again, "I want you to take your little brother into the toilet. Lock the door and stay in there until I come by for you. Mama will knock on the door three times in a row. Like this," she said, stopping for a moment and knocking on a sign on the wall and saying "Knock, knock, knock — three times in a row, like this—knock, knock, knock."

"What if someone else knocks?" I asked.

"Here we go with those questions again," Mama said. "No one else will knock *three* times like your Mama. If anyone else does knock, they'll just knock once or twice. No one knocks three times like this," she said, stopping again and knocking three times on another sign: *knock, knock, knock.*

"It's not likely anyone else will knock at all. If they do, don't open the door. Wait until you hear my three knocks, then come out right away and follow Mama."

"I hate to ask another question, Mama," I said, "but why do we have to go into the toilet?"

"It's Mama's train game. A train game is what it is, that's all. Why pay three train fares when one will get us to Yonkers the same way? The Grand Central Railroad has a lot more money than your Mama. They won't miss a few more pennies. Once the train starts, the conductor collects the tickets. When he takes my ticket, I'll come by the toilet for you. It's Mama's train game. You just do what your Mama says."

"I like games. It sounds like fun," my little brother said.

"It's more like being a stowaway," I said.

"What's a stow-way?" my little brother asked me.

"Stow-*a*-way," I said. "A stowaway is someone who hides some-place, so they won't have to pay the fare, right, Mama?"

"We'll be two toilet stow-ways," my little brother said laughing. "Toilet stow-ways. Toilet stow-ways."

Turning to me, Mama said, "You pick some funny times to teach your little brother new words. Some very funny times. Now as soon as we get on the train, go right in the toilet, do you hear?"

"Yes, Mama," I said.

"Stow-way, stow-way, stow-way," my little brother chanted.

"Shush!" Mama told him. "I don't want to hear that word come off your tongue again any more today. Be quiet now. As soon as we get on the train, go in the toilet with your brother. Don't for-get to lock the door," she reminded me.

The toilet was easy to find. I saw it the minute we boarded the train. Mama looked up and down the car to see if anyone was looking. No one was. Mama silently pointed to the door, and in we went.

The toilet was smaller than our bathroom at home. I didn't think anything could be more crowded than that, but this one was. I felt funny standing in the toilet with my little brother.

"How long do we have to stow-way here?" he asked.

"Shhh!" I said. "Mama told us to be quiet, and she told you *not* to use that word. We won't be in here too long. Do me a favor and don't use that word again. Mama will get very mad at the both of us if you say it again. Someone might hear you out there through the door. Everyone knows what that word means."

"I didn't!" my little brother said.

"Older people do, though. Now just be quiet so we can listen for Mama's knock."

Just as the train's engine began to sound and the train started to slowly move, there was a knock on the door.

One knock sounded and stopped. Then there were two knocks.

"Is that Mama already?" my little brother whispered.

"Shhh!" I said. "It can't be. Mama said she'd knock three times."

"Maybe she forgot."

"Shhh! Mama never forgets anything."

Two more knocks came again and stopped. I began to get scared. I knew it wasn't Mama. What if the train conductor was checking on stowaways? What if he found the two of us hiding out in there and threw us off the train? I prayed that Mama was close by.

"Anyone in there?" a lady's voice called.

I knew the voice wasn't Mama's, and I knew it wasn't the voice of the train conductor because all the conductors are men.

"Be right out," I called as quietly as I could so that hopefully only the lady would hear me.

"Take your time," the voice called back. "I'll go to the one in the next car."

Whew! I thought. That was close!

"Can stow-ways go to jail?" my little brother asked.

"Just be quiet. Please? Just be quiet until Mama knocks three times. And stop saying that word!"

Only a few minutes passed by after the lady's knock, but it seemed that my little brother and I had been shut up in this small toilet for a month. Was I glad when the *knock, knock, knock*—Mama's *knock, knock, knock*—finally sounded!

I opened the door carefully, went out first, and told my little brother to follow me. I saw Mama leaving her seat and walking through to the next car.

"Come on," I said. "Let's go. Quick!"

Before we caught up with her, Mama sat down.

"Well, here are my boys," Mama said, as we got to her seat, acting as if nothing had happened. "Let your little brother sit by the window. Sit next to him, and Mama will sit here on the end."

She placed a little pink piece of cardboard with holes punched out of it into a metal slit on the back of the seat in front of us.

"What's that for?" I asked.

"That's the ticket receipt," she answered. "The conductor gives you this when he takes your ticket."

The receipt read: GLAD TO HAVE YOU ABOARD! HOPE YOU WILL BE WITH US AGAIN SOON. PLEASE KEEP THIS CHECK IN SIGHT AND TAKE IT WITH YOU IF YOU LEAVE YOUR SEAT.

"Why did you change your seat?" I asked.

"No more questions. Just look out the window now. The train game's over! Just look out the window at the water. That's the Hudson River there. You'll ride up the Hudson River all the way to Yonkers. See the boats?"

"I'd like to go on a boat," my little brother said, without taking his eyes away from the window.

"Someday you will," Mama told him. "Someday you'll be big enough to do and have anything you want. Mama will see to that. My boys are going to have everything!"

"Here comes the conductor," I said.

"Gosh, are we there already?" my little brother asked.

"Not yet," Mama answered. "But we will be there soon. It's only a short ride to YONK-ers."

The conductor was walking up the aisle, looking at the little pink pieces of cardboard. When he got to our seat, he stopped, took Mama's pink piece of cardboard, and said, "Good afternoon."

"How many more stops is it to Yonkers?" Mama asked the conductor.

"Two more stops," he answered. "Ma'am, do you have your other receipts? I pick up the Yonkers receipts now."

We've had it, I thought, feeling the blood rush to my face. *We're going to be thrown off the train.*

"You just took it," Mama said calmly.

"And the boys' receipts?"

I knew we'd had it. Here it comes. And here we go!

"I changed my seat," Mama said, "because the other car was stuffy. Plain stuffy! The conductor in the other car said I could change cars if I took the receipts with me. The boys—you know how boys are—why, you're just a boy yourself. You know, you look just like my friend, Mr. Spencer. You look enough like him to be his son. Come to think of it, I haven't seen Mr. Spencer in quite a long time. Your last name isn't Spencer by any chance, is it?"

"No, ma'am," the conductor answered.

"What is your name?" Mama asked.

"Kelly," the conductor said.

"Kelly! Why that's a good Irish name. I bet your parents are proud of you. They should be proud as proud could be to have a good-looker like you for a son, plus a son who has a good job."

"Ma'am, I need the receipts," the conductor said, looking very impatient.

This is it, I thought again. I wondered what they did with train stowaways.

"Oh, *those* receipts," Mama said. "I started to say before your looks got me sidetracked, that you know how boys are."

I could tell Mama was thinking harder and harder.

"When we changed our seats—you see we were in the smoking car. I don't smoke, and it was so stuffy in there that the three of us just had to change our seats. All that smoking made our eyes water. I don't know how people can sit for so long in a car that's so filled with smoke, do you? You're lucky you're tending to this car. The air is cleaner here. You don't smoke, do you?"

"No ma'am," the conductor answered.

"That's wonderful. Just wonderful. Don't you ever start then. I always tell my boys never to start. If you don't start bad habits, you don't have to worry about stopping them. I always tell my boys to keep their bodies clean and healthy. Clean and healthy bodies equal clean and healthy minds. Anyway, I started to tell you about those receipts."

I really wondered how Mama was going to get out of this.

"When we changed our seats from the smoking car to this cleaner, fresh-airier one," she continued, "the boys stopped off at the facility. You know what I mean by the facility—the toilet? Well, those little devils had those receipts in their little hands, but you know how boys are. Sometimes they're mischievous. Why, they just went and flushed their receipts right down the facility."

My little brother looked at me. I looked at him as if to say, "Please don't say a word." He got the idea behind my look right away.

"O.K., ma'am," the conductor said, looking weary and holding the one receipt.

"You know how boys are," Mama repeated. "I hope it's no problem for you."

"No, ma'am. It's all right," he said, looking as if he wanted to get away from Mama as soon as he could—with or without the receipts.

No one said another word for the rest of the ride. Not even Mama. The three of us just sat, staring out of the window at the Hudson River.

"YUNK-ERS, next. YUNKERS. YUNKERS, next stop!" yelled

one of the other conductors.

My little brother bolted up out of his seat as if he had just gotten an electric shock.

"He said YUNK-ers, Mama. Did you hear him? He said YUNKERS."

"Mama doesn't care *what* he said. It's YONK! YONK-ers—not YUNK-ers. You say things the way your Mama tells you to say them. You listen to your Mama!"

As the train pulled to a stop, we got up and walked down the aisle to the door.

"Watch your step, please," the conductor said. "All off here for Yunkers."

"YONK!" Mama said to him. "Say YONK-ers. It's not YUNK. You're pronouncing it wrong."

"You're right, lady," the conductor said smiling.

"See," Mama said, turning to my little brother. "Mama's right. Even the train conductor of the railroad says so. You listen to your Mama, and you say things the way she tells you to say them. Your Mama's always right—most of the time. Take my hand now. Hold close together."

As soon as we walked out of the train, Mama saw Great-aunt Bertha standing near her car.

"Yoo-hoo-ooo!" Mama called. "Here we are. We made it. We're here."

We made it all right. But if the rest of the day was going to be anything like the train ride, I'd rather disappear right off the face of the earth!

Three

*"Everything new for my crew this year.
Everything new for my crew."*

"GOOD NIGHT," I SAID TO MY LITTLE BROTHER. "Good night, Mama."

"Good night," he answered. "Night, Mama."

"Good night to both of you, and don't let the bedbugs bite."

"Yuck!" my little brother squealed, moving down in his bed and pulling the blanket over his head.

Mama and I laughed. It always tickled us when he did this, and he knew it.

"See you both in the morning," Mama added, turning off the lights.

I wanted to go to sleep right away, but I couldn't. Thoughts of the day at Great-aunt Bertha's wouldn't let me. From the minute we got to her house, all she did was complain.

At one point, Great-aunt Bertha asked, "Are they the *best* suits the boys have?"

"What's wrong with those suits?" Mama snapped back. "They fit well."

"Oh, they do!" exclaimed Great-aunt Bertha. "But they *are* getting a little snug. Maybe I can help you out with some money to buy the boys new clothes."

"I'm doing fine," Mama said. "I have a good job. If there's any suit-buying to be done, *I'll* do it. I don't need any help!"

Even I got tired of all Great-aunt Bertha's gripes: *My little brother and I looked too skinny ... Mama looked tired out ... We're probably not eating well ... We must begin taking vitamin supplements ... The city is no place to raise two young children ... She hoped we were going to the dentist regularly ... We shouldn't watch too much TV ...*

She went on and on like that throughout the entire day. Instead of talking to Mama like a Mama, she talked to her like she was a little girl. At times I prayed for Great-uncle Albert to come to our rescue, maybe say something *nice* about us. But he hardly said a word.

In her own way, Mama got back at Great-aunt Bertha. Before we left her house, Great-aunt Bertha *insisted* that Mama take home one of her prize African violet plants.

"This will bring country sunshine into that cloudy city apartment you live in," said Great-aunt Bertha, tenderly wrapping the plant in aluminum foil and gently placing it in a plastic shopping bag.

As soon as we arrived back at Grand Central Terminal, Mama walked over to the first trash can she saw. Shaking the plastic bag, she hurled the African violet plant into the metal trash container with a thud!

"There! Any plant that flowers in the middle of the winter isn't normal. I wouldn't have that un-American thing in my house! This plastic shopping bag has more use to me," she said, folding it up and putting it under her arm.

My little brother and I were shocked. We never saw Mama throw *anything* away. But I was glad she did what she did. Great-aunt Bertha—and her plant—deserved it.

"When's Easter?" my little brother asked at breakfast.

"Soon," Mama answered. "Soon. The Easter Bunny will be here before you know it. He'll be bringing jelly beans and chocolate bunnies just three weeks from today. Besides jelly beans and chocolate bunnies, this year that old rabbit is also going to bring you and your brother brand-new Easter outfits. Everything new for my crew this year. Everything new for my crew."

I have to admit that Great-aunt Bertha *was* right about one thing—last year's Easter Sunday outfits were kind of snug. I guess that's the reason Mama feels we should have new dress-up clothes this year. But I wondered how Mama would be able to pay for two new Easter outfits.

Mama doesn't like questions, especially questions about money, so I wouldn't think of asking her. I knew she didn't have any money saved up. I knew because she was already two months past due on her tab at George's Grocery Store. I also knew that if she didn't pay him soon he was going to throw me out of the store the next time I went in and told him, "Mama said to put it on her tab."

George sells everything in his store. It's like a miniature supermarket. His prices are higher than any store around, but we buy most of our food there because Mama can put it on her tab and pay for it when she can. George is always nice to me—except when Mama doesn't pay him for months and her tab gets too high. When this happens I would rather die than go to George's. The one great thing about George, though, is that he never asks about Mama's tab when there are other customers in the store. He never tries to embarrass me.

When Mama can't pay him, she won't go near the store. But she does send me. She gives me a list of things to get and says, "Tell George to put it on Mama's bill. If Mama's out of sight, she's out of George's mind. If he doesn't see me, he can't ask about the money we owe him, can he? George would never turn you down, son. Never. You just tell him *Mama* said to put it on her tab. He won't give you any backtalk."

George never does refuse us anything. But Mama is wrong about her being out of his sight and mind. George is never as friendly when we owe him a lot of money as he is when we are all paid up. After I tell him what I want—what's on Mama's list —and tell him, "Mama said to put it on her tab," he looks at me icily, throws the things in a brown paper bag, and usually says something like, "You tell your Mama for me that I'd like to see her on Friday. *This* Friday. Your bill's getting too high again. I can't go on giving you credit if you don't pay up your bill. You tell your Mama that I have to pay up my bills or I'd go out of business. You tell her that for me."

And I say something short like, "Sure!" and flee the store as fast as I can. I hate those times.

Mama always does pay up when she has the money. I'm always glad to go to George's with Mama when we're going to pay our tab. George is always glad to see Mama march in the store. I think George can tell by the way Mama proudly struts through the door that she's come to pay.

On these times he lets me choose any candy bar I want to— free. I usually pick a Hershey bar with almonds.

"It's like getting interest in the bank account I have at school," I told Mama once.

"Don't you believe that," Mama said. "It's no interest at all. Not at all. It's his guilt coming out for overcharging us for everything in the first place. And for making you feel bad when I can't pay him. That's all it is. The candy bar is no interest. It's his guilt!"

The pay Mama earns at the department store is just barely enough to pay the rent, feed us, give me enough money to get back and forth from school, and pay Mrs. Rand, our upstairs neighbor, to watch my little brother when I'm at school.

How in the world is Mama going to get us new Easter outfits, too?

Four

"Even if your Mama has to sell chestnuts . . ."

MAMA WORKS EVERY WEDNESDAY NIGHT at the department store until nine. One Wednesday, after school, I went to the department store and met Mama for supper. She took me to a big cafeteria down the block, where I could pick out anything I wanted to eat. Mama always eats the same things for supper—a grilled cheese sandwich and a bowl of tomato soup with smashed-up crackers. Before Mama went back to the store, she gave me a shopping bag to take home.

"You take this bag right home and put it under Mama's bed. Don't open it up. Just put it under Mama's bed."

"What's in it?" I asked.

"Never mind what's in it. Do what your Mama says, and don't ask questions. You know your Mama doesn't like, questions—only answers. If I wanted you to know what's in it, I'd tell you, wouldn't I? Just go right home now and put the bag under Mama's bed."

I began doing this Wednesday after Wednesday—week after week. Most of the Wednesday bags were small and light. It was only early April, so it was too early for Mama to be Christmas shopping. I couldn't imagine what was in all those bags. But I did what she said—like always.

The last Wednesday before Easter Sunday, I took the bus uptown to the department store and, as usual, went to meet Mama for supper. I always waited for her at the toy store next to the department store because Mama told me not to come in. I figured that she didn't want me to see her working. Why? I don't know. It isn't always easy for me to figure out the things Mama says or does. I'd never ask. Even though I sometimes forget, I know Mama doesn't like me to ask her questions. Not at all!

At 6:30 Mama came by.

"You take this bag right home right now," she said, talking faster than ever and handing me a large, heavy, brown shopping bag. "Mama has no time for dinner tonight. No time at all. Mama has to rush right off—now! You go right home now," she said.

I never remembered Mama looking so nervous. She gave me a quick kiss on the cheek and disappeared into the crowd, saying again for the third time, "You go right home right now."

Everything seemed to happen so fast. One minute no Mama, the next minute Mama, and the next minute no Mama again. I was confused by Mama and also disappointed. I had come all the way from home, traveling over an hour to have dinner with her, and off she flew, without even telling me why. I felt bad all the way home. The heavy, bulky shopping bag I had to carry made me feel even worse.

Two stops before my house, I looked down into the bag. One package on the side of the shopping bag wasn't wrapped up like the others. I reached in and moved it up to see it better. It was undershorts—a package of three pairs of undershorts in *my* size.

When I got home, I put the bag under Mama's bed with all the other bags I had taken home on past Wednesday nights, and then I went upstairs to Mrs. Rand's to get my little brother.

I knocked on Mrs. Rand's door. She answered it.

"My, you're back early tonight," she said. "Come in. Did you meet your Mama?"

"Yes," I answered. "But Mama couldn't have dinner with me tonight 'cause the store was too busy and one of the girls was out sick. Mama's the only one in her department."

I *had* to tell her something like that. I couldn't tell her that Mama just ran off after shoving a shopping bag at me.

"Your poor Mama works far too hard and far too long," she said. "Do you want a hot dog? It'll only take a minute for me to make one for you."

"No, thank you, Mrs. Rand. I just came to get my little brother. I'll have something to eat downstairs."

I would have liked a hot dog. I was hungry. And I loved being with Mrs. Rand. She was one of my very best friends. But tonight I was worried about Mama. I just wanted to think about why Mama dashed away, and think about the heavy shopping bag I lugged home, and think about all the other bags that were under her bed. I wanted to think about Mama. I wanted to think.

My little brother came running from Mrs. Rand's living room.

"Hi," he said. "Want to play Old Maids?"

"Not now," I answered. "Let's go home. Bye, Mrs. Rand. Thanks for watching my little brother."

"No trouble at all. Tell your Mama I said hello when she comes home." Closing the door, I heard her say again, "That poor woman works far too hard and far too long."

The Saturday night before Easter Sunday, just before Mama was going to put my little brother to bed, she told us she had a big surprise.

"Come into Mama's room," she said. "Come in now."

Mama opened the door to her room and let us go in first. Laid out on her bed were piles of brand-new clothes: socks, pants, shirts, ties, pajamas—even suit jackets—for both my little brother and me.

I couldn't believe it. I really couldn't believe it. As I looked over everything, my eyes suddenly stopped on the undershorts. There they were—the undershorts in my size that had been shoved in the shopping bag Mama'd given me to take home last Wednesday.

"I told you. I told you you'd have new Easter outfits. Mama told you there'd be everything new for my crew this year, didn't she? Everything new for my crew," she said, smiling and smiling.

Mama certainly had told us that. My little brother and I probably had the newest outfits of any kid on our block—right down to the undershorts.

"You help your little brother take the clothes to your room. Hang up the pants and jackets so they'll be fresh tomorrow morning. Mama wants you both to look nice. Fresh and nice and new. As fresh and new as Easter morning," she said, still smiling and smiling.

34

As I looked over all the clothes on Mama's bed, a thought raced through my mind—that Mama's bed looked too much like the boys' clothing section of the department store where she worked. I gathered up the clothes—just like Mama said—and took them to our room.

As I was turning out all of the lights in our bedroom, Mama walked in.

"I have something to tell the both of you before you go to sleep. Something new and exciting. I'm not going back to the department store on Monday. Mama quit! Starting on Monday, your Mama's going to have a new job working for Mr. Dakin, the butcher, and his wife. I'm going to be their housekeeper. Mrs. Dakin is matching the pay I get at the department store and even giving me extra for cooking their dinner. How about that? Mama won't have to work anymore on Wednesday nights *or* Saturdays. This is a nine-to-five job with weekends off. O-f-f. We'll have more time to be together now."

I wasn't surprised that Mama was quitting her job at the department store. It seems like Mama's worked at a million jobs. Once she was a waitress in a diner, but that only lasted two weeks because Mama felt sorry for anybody that looked like they couldn't afford the prices. One night the man who owned the place caught her charging an old lady twenty cents for a hamburger deluxe when it should have been a dollar and a quarter.

Another time, Mama worked in an ice-cream parlor, but she was fired from that job because she put too much ice cream in the dishes after she was told not to. Mama didn't agree with the owner of the place. She told him he was stingy and that kids, especially, should get more ice cream for the high prices he charged. The man didn't like her talking back to him that way and asked her to leave. She did!

I can't even remember how many jobs Mama has had. The department store job is the only one where Mama stayed more than a couple of months. It was the first job she took after Dad walked out on us.

"Just because your old man left us is no reason why we won't make it through," Mama often told us. "You know your Mama never likes to say anything bad about people, but any man that would leave his wife and two fine, young boys is no good with a capital N.G. But we'll make it, sons. You'll see. Even if your Mama has to sell chestnuts out on the street in front of St. Patrick's Cathedral in the cold and dark of winter, we'll make it through. Just have faith in your Mama."

My little brother was too young to know what Mama was talking about. But *I* knew. I always had faith in Mama. I had good reason to.

I never saw Mama smile such a big smile as when Reverend Goodbar told us after the Easter Sunday church service that we were the handsomest family at church. Mama sure was proud of that. My little brother and I were, too.

"You remind Mama to scrape up an extra dollar to put in the church envelope the next time we come here, son. That Reverend Goodbar's a good man. He knows quality—in people and in clothing. He sure knows quality, that man."

I hated to take my Easter outfit off that night. I stood in front of the bathroom mirror for tons of minutes just looking at myself in my new clothes. In bed, I worried and wondered how Mama could possibly afford to dress us like she did today.

Sometimes I think I know. Sometimes I'm sure I know. But I'd rather not think such things—especially about Mama.

Five

"Mrs. Dakin had one left over this month."

MAMA BEGAN WORKING FOR MRS. DAKIN AS A HOUSEKEEPER on Easter Monday, just as she told us she would.

Mrs. Dakin is a busy woman. She is always gardening, playing golf, or going to some kind of church meeting. I told Mama I was glad she was working for Mrs. Dakin because now she didn't have to work nights or Saturdays. I also told Mama that I was glad she was working for Mrs. Dakin because Mrs. Dakin was nice.

"Nice? Nice? You toss the word 'nice' around too much, especially when you talk about people. You know that your Mama likes people very much—all kinds of people. Mama likes people whether they're black, white, red, or yellow, but they're not all nice! There's good and bad of all kinds, and don't you ever forget that."

"I know that, but what does that have to do with Mrs. Dakin? I think she's nice. She's nice to me."

"Nice, nice, nice. You don't know what nice is. You know your Mama never likes to say anything bad about people, but Mrs. Dakin isn't so nice. She's a dumb woman. And dumb isn't nice."

"Why is she dumb, Mama?" I asked.

"I'll tell you why she's dumb. She's ashamed of her husband being a butcher. Can you imagine that? Instead of being happy with a man who cuts meat for a living, she's ashamed of him. So she tries to be someone she isn't, like a fancy social butterfly. All day long she flitters and flutters around trying to make impressions on people as though she was a movie star or something. I think she thinks that if she flitters and flutters around long enough, people will forget she's married to a butcher. There's nothing wrong with a man butchering for a living, except in that sick mind of hers. With the prices of meat being what they are today, she should consider herself proud to be married to a butcher.

"She doesn't make an impression on your Mama, though, none at all. Your Mama knew that woman was dumb the first time I laid eyes on that house of hers."

"What does her house have to do with being dumb?" I interrupted.

"Any woman who doesn't know about her own house is dumb. Why, she can't even clean. She doesn't know her Comet from her Mr. Clean. She can't cook either. Mrs. Mahler, who lives next door to her, told me that she burns everything—even chicken. Any woman who burns a chicken is really dumb. Yesterday I asked her about a scorched pan she left in the greasy sink. Do you know what she told me? She told me she burned it making soft-boiled eggs for Mr. Dakin's breakfast on Sunday! How could anyone scorch a pan making *soft*-boiled eggs! I said it before, and I'll say it again, son, your Mama never likes to say anything bad about people, but Mrs Dakin is dumb!"

One afternoon, soon after Mama began working for Mrs. Dakin, she phoned home.

"Son? This is your Mama here, hear? Did you peel the potatoes yet?" she asked.

"Yes, Mama," I said. "I'm putting them on at six o'clock, like you told me to."

"Good. Put them on at six o'clock like I told you to. But leave the chipped beef in the refrigerator. We're having steak for supper tonight. I'll bring it home with me and broil it as soon as I get home."

"Steak?" I asked, surprised.

"Yes, steak. What's the matter with you? You never heard of steak before? It's the part of the bull you eat. I'm bringing home a steak from Mrs. Dakin. She had one left over this month. I'll be home by six-thirty. Say hello to your little brother for me, and give him a kiss, hear? Tell him we're having steak for supper. Mama has to go now. Bye, bye."

Mama hung up.

Steak! We haven't had steak for ages. But, oh, do we have chipped beef and potatoes. We have it several times a week—plain with boiled potatoes, creamed on toast, and plain mixed in with mashed potatoes. But steak! Just the thought of it made my mouth juices flow.

I raced into our bedroom and shouted to my little brother, "Steak! Mama's bringing home a steak for supper tonight."

"Do you want to play Old Maids with me?" he calmly asked.

I just looked at him. I couldn't get mad because he probably didn't remember what steak was. *I* could hardly remember it.

Besides cleaning the Dakins' house and cooking dinner for them, part of Mama's job was to order all their meat. She got deliveries from Mr. Dakin's butcher shop once a month. He was always so busy in his shop, and Mrs. Dakin was always so busy trying to be somebody she wasn't, that neither of them kept track of anything—but Mama did. She knew every ounce of meat that went into their freezer!

Once Mama began working for the Dakins, dinners at our house got better and better. My school lunches did, too! Instead of peanut butter and jelly sandwiches in my lunchbox, there were thick, broiled chicken legs; instead of baloney sandwiches, sirloin steak found its way between slices of bread.

It wasn't long before Mama began bringing home chickens, pork chops, lamb chops, hams, roast beefs, and steaks nearly every single night. Our refrigerator was bursting with meat. We hardly had enough room to fit a container of milk in it anymore. We were eating so much good meat that my little brother and I began missing the old chipped beef and potatoes menu.

One night after supper, while Mama was cleaning out the refrigerator, she said to me, "Son, do me a favor and take this roast beef upstairs to Mrs. Rand. There's no room in here for it. She probably hasn't had a good piece of meat like this in years. She's on food stamps, you know. People like her who have to use those things can't afford to waste them on cuts of meat like this."

"What are food stamps?" my little brother asked.

"They're little pieces of paper the government gives to some people each month. They're like money. You exchange them for food."

"Why don't we get some?" he asked.

"Because *we're not some people*, that's why! Mama's not a food stamp kind of woman. Mama doesn't like charity of any kind. Not as long as I'm able to work and provide for us. Food stamps are for those who can't find decent jobs or for older people who just can't make a living. I'll tell you one thing: Food stamps can buy chicken livers and that mushy scrapple made from pork scrap and cornmeal that a lot of people eat to survive on—but they don't buy roast beefs like this one.

"Now go on, son," she said to me. "Take this up to Mrs. Rand. Tell her I had an extra one."

Whenever I asked Mama about all the extra meat we had stuffed in the refrigerator, she told me the same thing: "Mrs. Dakin had one left over this month."

It didn't take me long to figure out that if Mrs. Dakin did "have *one* left over this month" of all the different types of meat Mama brought home, Mama would have had to work for the Dakins for several years instead of just several months. Mrs. Dakin would never give away so much meat. I knew she wouldn't and didn't.

When Mama brought home *two* turkeys for our Thanksgiving Day dinner, I was convinced she was getting more out of this job than just her weekly pay. I was sure Mama was taking the meat— almost positive! I think she took all those new Easter clothes from the boys' section of the department store, too.

If Mama was taking the Dakins' meat, I'd rather have the old chipped beef than a hundred steaks or a hundred of any kind of meat. I don't want Mama to do anything wrong. I don't want anything to happen to Mama!

Six

"What do you think your Mama is—a dictionary?"

THE SUNDAY AFTER THANKSGIVING, while all three of us were sitting around looking at the Sunday papers, my little brother showed Mama an advertisement for a Christmas tree. Even though the ad was black and white, the tree was beautiful—covered with balls, tinsel, and candy canes, sparkling from its skinny top to its fat bottom.

"Mama, can we have a pretty Christmas tree this year? Can we have one like this one?" he asked, handing her the newspaper. "Can we, Mama? Can we?"

Mama looked at the ad, thought for a moment or two, and said, "You sure can. And you sure will! But your tree will be much prettier than *this* spindly-looking thing. Much prettier. You'll see. Leave it to your Mama!"

I was surprised to hear Mama say that. I figured our tree would be the same as last year, and the year before, and the year before that. Our tree is always the same.

Each year Mama takes us up to George's Grocery Store to pick it out. Every Christmas Eve, right before George closes his store, Mama bundles up my little brother and me and all three of us walk to George's to get our Christmas tree. Mama says this is the best time to go because the trees are cheaper. George has to sell them for what he can get for them.

"They're no good to him on Christmas Day," Mama says. "No good at all. He could take those leftover trees one by one and shove them! You know your Mama never likes to say anything bad about people, but that crook will charge us at least a dollar for a tree he gets stuck with. A dollar for something that's not even worth a dime tomorrow morning. Not even worth one dime."

I don't agree with Mama about this. I never did. The leftover trees are good enough for me. They *are* the trees that nobody else wants, but they're trees—real, live trees. Most of them are picked over. Some of them have branches torn off, and some have needles that fall off like a needle-storm the second you pick them up. Others look scrubby, straggly, stunted, and shabby. But if you look them over—each and every one—you can find a good one. It's sort of like playing a game to see how good a tree we can find. Even a real scrubby, straggly, stunted, or shabby tree is better than an artificial tree. I don't think a dollar is too much to pay for a tree, even a picked-over one.

When we do find a tree, we take it home and trim it with paper chains I made at school when I was in the first grade, the box of red and green Christmas balls Mama keeps in her closet from year to year, and pretend-snow made from cotton balls.

When we're all finished, the tree always looks underdressed. Many Christmases I thought our tree would have looked better if we hadn't trimmed it—just left it a tree tree. No tree we ever had ever looked like the one in the ad my little brother showed Mama. Ours always looked worse in living color than this ad did in black and white!

Mama said, though, that this year the tree would be pretty. Even prettier than the one in the ad. One thing I knew for sure— what Mama says, Mama does. Always!

A week after my little brother had asked Mama about the tree, we were in the middle of dinner when Mama said, "Your Mama has something to tell the both of you. Something new and exciting."

Uh-oh, I thought to myself. What now? When Mama starts off with, "Your Mama has something to tell the both of you. . . ," it usually means she's quitting her job again. I can tell by the tone of her voice and the look in her eyes.

"Your Mama's decided to quit working as Mrs. Dakin's house-keeper. I've been there too long. Too long. Mama's tired of scrubbing old Dakin's filthy floors and washing her dirty windows and cooking for her and her crabby old husband. Your Mama's going to start working in the five-and-ten-cent store tomorrow morning—the big five-and-ten-cent store downtown right in the middle of the city. I was down at the five-and-ten-cent store last week doing some shopping, and do you know who I bumped into there?"

"Who?" I asked.

"Dotty Schmidt."

"Who's Dotty Schmidt?" my little brother asked, cutting into one of the biggest, thickest pork chops I had ever seen in my whole life—one right out of Mrs. Dakin's freezer and into Mama's frying pan!

"You don't know who she is," Mama answered. "She used to work with your Mama at the department store. She was in panty hose."

My little brother started laughing.

"What's the matter with you?" Mama asked.

"Is that all she had on?" said my little brother, laughing louder.

I laughed, too.

"That's enough of this silliness," Mama said. "Mama doesn't like silly talk at the dinner table. Dotty Schmidt *sold* panty hose at the department store. Anyway, I haven't seen Dotty Schmidt since I left the department store last April after Easter—before I went to work for those crabby Dakins. You never know people until you've worked for them. Never! Dotty Schmidt left the department store, too. Now she's working at the five-and-ten-cent store selling candy.

"I was on my way out of the five-and-ten-cent store and just happened to be walking past the candy counter when I heard a voice calling me. Sure enough, there was Dotty Schmidt standing behind the gumdrops. Why, it was like we just saw one another yesterday. Your Mama always liked Dotty Schmidt. I started talking with her, and she told me how much she loved working in the five-and-ten-cent store. The store is very busy now with Christmas here full blast. Everyone is out spending their money—the money they save all year long to spend at Christmastime. Dotty told me the store was hiring a lot of extra help because they were so busy.

"That's when your Mama got an idea. If the five-and-ten-cent store was hiring a lot of extra people to work for Christmas, why shouldn't your Mama work there, too, especially since Dotty Schmidt talked so well about her job?"

"If they're only hiring people for Christmas, what will you do after Christmas, Mama?" I asked. "Christmas only lasts for a few more weeks —until December 24th."

"Your Mama knows when Christmas is. Your Mama's been around to see more Christmases than you have. I'll think about after Christmas *after* Christmas! Your Mama's a good worker. Places don't let the good workers go so fast. Good workers like your Mama bring in the customers, and customers bring in money to spend, and spent money equals profits. That's the way all businesses run.

"Besides, if they do lay me off after Christmas, I can always find another job. Mama has faith, and you have faith in your Mama. I'll always find a way to get us through. I always have, and I always will.

"Now what was I saying? You made me forget."

"I'm sorry, Mama," I said. "You were talking about Dotty Schmidt."

"Oh, yes. Dotty Schmidt. Well, right there on the spot I got the idea to apply for a job at the five-and-ten-cent store, and I told Dotty Schmidt about it. She told me I could use her name as a reference for a job."

"What's a reference?" my little brother asked.

"What do you think your Mama is—a dictionary? Do I look like a dictionary? You ask too many questions at the dinner table. I don't like to hear so many questions when we're eating. Mama's trying to explain something. I can't explain something to you if you keep asking questions, can I?"

"No, Mama," my little brother answered. "I'm sorry."

"As I was trying to say, Dotty Schmidt told me I could use her name as a reference."

Turning to my little brother, Mama said, "A reference is when someone says something good about your character to the someone in charge of something so you can get what you're trying for."

"Oh," my little brother mumbled, still working on his pork chop.

"So I marched right up to the personnel office," Mama continued, "the place where they hire people for the store. I filled out all the forms and before I knew it, in just a few minutes, I was told by the woman in charge that I had a job and that I could start work right away. I told Mrs. Dakin that I was leaving the very next day. I don't think she liked it one little bit, but your Mama can't worry about people the likes of those Dakins. Let them find someone else to be their slave. That's what your Mama feels like, working for those two—a slave. Your Mama's better than a slave, and your Mama deserves more out of life than putting up with the likes of people like those two."

"I thought you liked Mrs. Dakin, Mama," I said. "Look at all the good meat she's given us. We never had so much good meat before in our lives."

"This pork chop's real good," my little brother said.

"We did without good meat before, and we'll do without it again. What would you rather have—good meat or a happy Mama? Mama doesn't want to talk anymore about Mr. Dakin, Mrs. Dakin, or their meat. I start work at the five-and-ten-cent store tomorrow morning. And that's what your Mama is going to think about."

I wanted so much to talk to Mama about the meat. I wanted to find out from Mama herself where it had really come from. I was going to try once and for all.

"Mama," I started, "can we talk about all the meat you've been bringing home?"

"Maybe your ears need to be cleaned out. Maybe you didn't hear your Mama, son. I just got done saying that I don't want to talk about Mr. Dakin, Mrs. Dakin, or their meat. Did you hear that? Mama's tired of meat. Starting tomorrow morning, I begin working in the five-and-ten-cent store—at the Christmas ornament counter."

Oh, no, I thought. The Christmas ornament counter! All of a sudden the luxurious-looking Christmas tree my little brother showed Mama in the ad flashed in my brain like a magic vision!

"Mr. Dakin, Mrs. Dakin, and their meat are past now," Mama continued. "People should forget the past. Only think about right now and think about tomorrow. The past is past, but the future is the future. Now finish your dinner. Eat! Let's not talk anymore about Mr. Dakin, Mrs. Dakin, or their meat. Mama's sick and tired of meat. Eat!"

Seven

"Mama's in Christmas ornaments."

MAMA TOOK THE BUS BACK AND FORTH to work every day. If it wasn't too cold outside, or if Mama didn't have to work too late, my little brother and I met her at the bus stop. Sometimes we had to wait for bus after bus. If Mama wasn't on the first bus, we'd both be a little disappointed. But when she finally came, it was well worth the waiting for. Then the three of us would walk home together while Mama told us about her day at work.

One day, in the middle of December, I was getting ready for school when Mama said, "You take this money. There's enough bus fare to get to the city and back, and fifteen cents extra. You come down to the store after school between six and six-thirty tonight. Mama's in Christmas ornaments. You'll see the counter right as you get off the down escalator. Pretend you don't know me—like you never saw me before, hear? Ask Mama for one box of Christmas ball hangers. They're fifteen cents. And don't ask for another thing. Just one box of Christmas ball hangers. When I give them to you in a bag, leave the store right away and come right back home. Put the bag under Mama's bed. It's a game we're playing, hear? A game."

Oh, no, I thought, shuddering inside, remembering the Yonkers train game and the Easter outfit games I had played with her, *and* the Dakins' meat game she'd played by herself.

"Mama," I said, "I can't come to the store tonight. I have to study my part in the Christmas pageant at school."

"What Christmas pageant at school? You didn't tell me about any school pageant. You know your Mama is interested in what you do at school. If you're in some kind of play—especially some kind of pageant-play, your Mama should know about it. Haven't I always come to see you in school plays, ever since the day you played the troll in *The Three Billy Goats Gruff* in kindergarten? Even if I have to take a few hours off from work without pay, I always want to see you in school plays. Your Mama always made a practice of that. Always! And I always will."

Knowing I was trapped in my own lie because there really wasn't a school pageant, I said, "This is only a little pageant, Mama. No parents are invited. It's only for the other kids to see."

"Sounds stupid to me," Mama said. "If you're going through all the trouble of having a pageant—and especially if you're in it—

the parents should be notified with a written invitation so they can see it performed. You know your Mama never likes to say anything bad about people, but those people who run the schools nowadays don't think as good as they used to. Schools used to invite parents to see *all* the plays their kids were in. Now all they do is invite parents to stupid P.T.A. meetings where they have speakers who put the whole auditorium to sleep.

"The last time I went to one of those P.T.A. meetings there was a doctor who talked for over an hour about teeth problems. And there wasn't even one teacher there—not even your own teacher. When I take the time to go to school, I want to hear your teacher tell me how fine you're doing, not hear someone talk about teeth. Mama wants to hear about your mind. The dentist can take care of your teeth. That new principal they got in last year spends more of his time making believe he's a principal than principaling. He should invite parents to see their children in plays once in a while. Especially pageant-plays. That's what he should do. Or he should go. Right out with the garbage.

"Anyway, what does all this have to do with your coming down to the five-and-ten-cent store today after school?"

"Well," I stammered, "I really have to study my part."

"What part are you playing in the pageant that your Mama *hasn't* been invited to?"

I had to think quickly. "I'm playing one of the Wise Men, Mama," I said.

"The Wise Men?" Mama asked. "What Wise Man? What do you have to study if you're playing one of the Wise Men? They didn't say anything. All they did was look at the star and head over to Bethlehem with their gifts for the baby Jesus. I never remember any of them saying anything. Nothing at all. The reason they were called the Wise Men is because they kept their mouths shut.

Wise people don't go around talking so much when something big is happening. The Wise Men knew they couldn't compete with the birth of Jesus. If they did say anything, they might have been written right out of the Bible and no one would ever have heard of them. Your Mama never remembers any of them saying anything."

"In our pageant they do," I answered sheepishly.

"With that new principal, anything is possible, I guess. He even thinks he can rewrite the Bible! You can study your part after school, and you can study it on the bus coming and going. But you're *coming* to the five-and-ten-cent store tonight. Between six and six-thirty. Remember now, Mama's downstairs in Christmas ornaments right as you get off the down escalator. Ask me for one box of Christmas ball hangers. Just ball hangers. Take them and come right back home. You'll have plenty of time to study your Wise Man part. Remember. It's a game we're playing. A game."

"Can't you bring the ball hangers home with you?" I asked.

"How many times have I told you that your Mama doesn't like questions? Only answers. Now just do what I say."

That evening I brought my little brother upstairs to Mrs. Rand's, took the bus into the city, went to the five-and-ten-cent store, took the down escalator downstairs, and found the Christmas ornament counter right where Mama said it would be. The counter wasn't busy, and I saw Mama right away. It was funny seeing her behind a store counter. It was even funnier pretending she wasn't my Mama. But I did what she said.

I walked up to the counter, picked up a box of Christmas ball hangers, and handed it to Mama. Mama took a giant bag from underneath the counter and kept saying things like:

"You want eight of these?"—putting plastic candy canes into

the bag. "Oh, you want a box of these?"—throwing in red and green, round and shiny, glass ornaments. And: "This is a nice nativity set you picked out. Here's Joseph and Mary and baby Jesus in his crib. Of course you'll want some lambs and cows and donkeys. And a couple of camels."

Moving over to another area of the counter she continued:

"And Wise Men. Christmas wouldn't be Christmas without the Wise Men, would it?"

Then she asked out of the side of her mouth like a gangster in an old TV movie, "Which one are you playing in the pageant?"

"This one," I answered, pointing my shaking finger at the one carrying frankincense and feeling more guilty than ever for lying to Mama.

"Well, you'll want two of those then, won't you?" she asked, stuffing them and some other things into the bag.

Mama was stuffing and stuffing. I thought I'd die. Right there on the spot. Right in front of all the Christmas ornaments.

Mama finally handed the bag over the counter to me. It was almost as big as I was. I handed Mama the fifteen cents, which was as wet as Niagara Falls from the sweat that had filled the palm of my quaking hand.

"Thank you. That's just the right change. Thank you, young man," Mama said, like she never saw me before in her whole life. "Merry, merry Christmas to you."

I couldn't move. I just stood there frozen!

Bending over the counter, Mama said, "Get out of here. Get right home like I told you to!"

Turning to a customer, Mama smiled a great big smile and said, "Merry Christmas. Can I help you, ma'am?"

I knew what Mama was doing—what Mama did. Mama was stealing all those Christmas things, and I was helping her do it.

This whole thing seemed like an awful TV show.

I quickly got my senses together—and my legs—and made a dash to the up escalator. Thank God the Christmas ornament counter was close by or I might never have made it. As the escalator carried me upstairs, I looked around to see if there was a police officer around to put me away for good. There wasn't. I walked out of the store trying hard not to drop the big, bulky bag of Christmas things. I grabbed the bus home as fast as I could.

I couldn't imagine why Mama was doing what she was doing. But I knew one thing. I didn't like it at all.

That wasn't the last of the Christmas "game" I had to play at the five-and-ten. Most days I was able to convince Mama that I had things to do for school. But other times, Mama just wouldn't take any excuse. So I ended up making a few more trips during December.

We did the same thing each time. I was almost getting used to the routine, but I was always just as scared. It made me feel ashamed of myself, too—and ashamed of Mama.

The one thing that *really* frightened me was a sign on the front door of the five-and-ten-cent store that read: WARNING: SHOPLIFTING IS A CRIMINAL OFFENSE. SHOPLIFTERS WILL BE PROSECUTED.

The very worst day—the worst day of my whole life—was the Wednesday before Christmas. I made my usual pilgrimage downtown to the five-and-ten-cent store, walked through the door with that sign, and took the down escalator to the Christmas ornament counter. Halfway down the escalator I saw Mama waiting on a woman, *and* I saw the other clerk behind the counter also waiting on someone.

The store was bursting with people, and Mama's counter

seemed the busiest. By the time the escalator landed, I didn't know what to do. Mama had told me if I ever came to the store and saw someone else behind the counter to wait only for her. So I casually walked along the counter so that Mama could see me and then strolled over to the next aisle, aisle eight, the hardware section.

I kept trying to look at Mama out of the corner of my eye. As soon as I saw that she was finished with the customer, I made a quick dash to the Christmas ornaments.

I did my usual bit—walked over, picked up still another box of Christmas ball hangers (we now had more ball hangers than balls), and handed it to Mama.

At that very moment, Mama looked up, looked at me, looked up again, looked at me again, turned as red as the reddest Christmas balls, shoved the ball hangers—and still another Wise Man—into a small bag, took the fifteen cents, leaned over the counter, and said, "Get going. Quick! The store detective's coming down the escalator!"

Then, without a word of warning, Mama threw up her arms and screamed, "Oh, my God. A mouse! A mouse! I think I saw a mouse in that tinsel box! I think I'm going to faint!"

The entire place seemed to stop—except for me. I knew that was my cue to start. Clutching the tiny bag of ball hangers and the one Wise Man, I made a quick dash to the up escalator, and up, up, and away I went through the door with the sign blaring: WARNING: SHOPLIFTING IS A CRIMINAL OFFENSE. SHOPLIFTERS WILL BE PROSECUTED.

I didn't want to think that I was shoplifting, but I *was* shoplifting; so was Mama. The two of us were stealing things—really stealing all of these Christmas things from the five-and-ten-cent store.

On the way home I prayed and prayed for Christmas to come faster. I couldn't go through any more of this five-and-ten-cent store game. I just couldn't. This was one of the very worst games Mama ever played. It wasn't really a game at all. It was far too real.

When I got home I put the small bag—the smallest one I ever carried home—under Mama's bed, the way I had all the times before. There was hardly any room left under there. There were bags galore—big ones, small ones, medium-sized ones—more bags than I had brought home. It looked like a bag factory!

If the police came in and saw all this stuff, we'd all get sentenced to at least ten years in jail.

Going upstairs to Mrs. Rand's to get my little brother, I couldn't help wondering what it would be like to spend Christmas inside a jail cell.

In bed that night, when I closed my eyes, all I could see was the sign on the five-and-ten-cent store door—WARNING: SHOPLIFTING IS A CRIMINAL OFFENSE. SHOPLIFTERS WILL BE PROSECUTED. The words wouldn't go out of my mind no matter how hard I tried to forget about them.

Eight

"Mama wants you to keep on smiling all through your life."

I WAITED UNTIL MY LITTLE BROTHER WENT TO BED so that I could be alone with Mama. I didn't know how to even begin talking to her about what I wanted to talk with her about.

"You're quiet tonight, son," Mama said. "I suppose with Christmas just a few days away, you've got those visions of sugarplums dancing around in your head. Your little brother does, bless his heart. Mama can tell. She can almost see those visions of sugarplums dancing around in his head. Is that why you're so quiet tonight?"

"No, Mama. It's not visions of sugarplums that are on my mind right now. It's something else. It's something I want to talk with you about."

"Well, let's talk then. Tell your Mama what you want to talk about. You can talk to your Mama about anything, you know that. If a son can't talk to his Mama—especially when he has no daddy around to talk to—who can he talk to? Tell Mama what's on your mind."

Since Mama seemed willing to talk for a change, I decided to start. "Mama," I began, "I don't like the five-and-ten-cent store game we're playing."

"Well, if that's what you want to talk to your Mama about, there's nothing to talk about. We're through with that game. All through. So there's nothing to talk about. Not at all. That game's over now!"

"But what about the game so far? What about all those things you gave me to take home from the ornament counter? Mama, we didn't pay for any of those things. The fifteen cents you give to me and I give to you at the store is only enough to pay for *one* box of Christmas ball hangers. What about the tons of other stuff I took from the store?"

"I *said* I didn't want to talk about the five-and-ten-cent store game anymore. Your Mama loves you and your little brother more than anything in the world. You know how much your Mama loves Christmas, don't you? Well, I don't love Christmas even one-tenth of the way I love you and your little brother."

"But—," I started.

"No more 'buts'. Butt yourself into bed now. Mama doesn't want you to think about the five-and-ten-cent store game any-more. It's past now. Mama told you that the five-and-ten-cent store game is over—through. Past is past. Only think about now. Think about yourself and where you are right now, and think about tomorrow.

"I'm going to bed now. Standing behind the counter for eight hours a day makes Mama's legs sore. I'm too tired to talk anymore tonight. The store is crowded these last few days before Christmas. It gets more and more crowded every single day. Everyone waits until the last minute to buy their tree ornaments. The store looks like an overcrowded baseball stadium all day long. The work is hard at the store, harder than any job your Mama's ever had.

"All the girls complain about how tired their legs are. Even Dotty Schmidt told me just yesterday, when we had a lunch break together, how tired out her legs get standing up eight hours a day. All the girls at the store complain about their legs. Sometimes we all sound like a TV commercial. Mama's going to bed now. Make sure you turn off all the lights before you go to bed, hear? Con Edison gets enough of Mama's hard-earned money. I only hope Con Edison—whoever he is—has to pay his own gas and electric bills. Maybe he'll figure out that the people who run his company have no right to be charging such high prices for something everyone needs and just has to use. Didn't Thomas Edison invent the light bulb?"

"Yes, Mama," I answered, knowing I wasn't going to get anywhere trying to talk to her. When Mama doesn't want to talk about something, she won't. Instead, she talks about other things —about anything that comes into her mind, anything but the thing I really want to talk with her about.

"Well, that Thomas Edison must just toss around and around in his grave every time Con Edison sends out a bill. I wonder if Con is related to Thomas? No matter who Con is, if Thomas knew what they were going to end up charging for the use of his invention, he never would've invented it. He was supposed to be a good man, you know. I read that somewhere. If he could come back today, even *he* couldn't afford to use electricity. Can you imagine that? The man who invented the light bulb wouldn't be able to afford to use it. These are crazy times we're living in, son, just crazy as crazy could be. Whenever your Mama thinks that things just can't get any crazier in this world, they do!"

I could tell by the tone of Mama's voice and the way she was beating around the bush and the way she looked up from her newspaper now and then that she knew I was upset by the five-and-ten-cent store game. I think she knew that I knew everything.

Sometimes I really can't figure Mama out, as hard as I try to. Either she was too embarrassed to talk with me or she really does believe that "past is past" stuff. One thing I know for sure—when Mama doesn't want to talk about something, she won't, no matter how hard you try to get her to. It was hopeless. I knew I'd have to wait for another time to talk to Mama.

Mama dropped the newspaper, got up, and walked over to me.

"Good night, son," she said, kissing me on the cheek.

"Good night, Mama."

As she started walking out of the living room, I asked, "Aren't you going to say it, Mama?"

"Say what?"

"What you always say before we go to bed."

"Oh . . . sleep tight and don't let the bedbugs bite."

Mama laughed. I smiled.

"Your Mama likes to see you smiling. Mama wants you to keep on smiling all through your life. You keep smiling."

She walked over and took me in her arms.

"I don't want you to think anymore about the past, O.K., son? You have faith in your Mama. Always. If you lose faith in your Mama, Mama's life won't be worth anything at all. Now good

60

night. And *don't* let those bedbugs bite, you hear?"

Mama wiped away a tear that rolled down her cheek. I gave her an extra-hard squeeze to let her know how much I loved her. I guess life isn't easy for her all the time. Not easy at all.

I had to talk to someone about Mama. But who could I talk to? My little brother wouldn't understand. Even if he could, I wouldn't want to tell him about Mama. I wouldn't want him to know what either of us was doing. I knew I shouldn't talk to anyone at school about her. And I knew I couldn't talk to Mama about Mama, not after tonight. She'd pretend not to listen, and I'd only make her sad.

All night long I thought and thought about who I could talk to. I decided there was only one person—Mrs. Rand. I decided that I would talk to her the next day, right after school, when I went upstairs to pick up my little brother.

The next day, when I got home, I went right upstairs and knocked on Mrs. Rand's door.

"Who's there?" she called.

"It's me, Mrs. Rand," I answered.

"Come in," she said. "Door's open. I'm in the kitchen."

As I opened the door, my little brother ran to me.

"Hi! Want to play Old Maids with me?"

"Not now. I'll play later. I promise."

Mrs. Rand laughed. "That little brother of yours is an Old Maids freak. I've played at least five games with him today. And I always lose. If ever there's an Old Maids tournament in the U.S. Olympics, your little brother is goin' to win all the gold medals. He's better at that game than Mark Spitz is at swimmin'."

I laughed, too.

"Have some milk and cookies," Mrs. Rand said. "I just made

these cookies. I've been makin' them at Christmastime since I was a little girl. The recipe's one that my mother got from her mother. It's been in the family for years and years and years. There's nothin' like fresh Christmas cookies."

"Mrs. Rand?" I asked. "Can I talk to you about something?"

"You know you can," she said, pouring a glass of milk for me and my little brother. "You can talk to me about anythin' that's on your mind. I'm a good listener. My husband, rest his soul, always said that to me. He'd tell me, 'Honey,' he always called me that, 'most people just talk and talk and never say a thing. But you listen more than you talk, and your listenin' says more than a lot of people's words do.' Eli was a great man. It's a shame you never knew him. You and he would've gotten along well together. So would your little brother and him. He liked card games, too."

"When are you going to play Old Maids with me?" my little brother interrupted.

"Later," I said. "Downstairs. I promise."

"Why don't you take your milk and cookies and go watch the television set?" Mrs. Rand said to him. "Your brother and I want to visit for a while."

"O.K.," my little brother said, taking his milk and cookies and disappearing into the living room.

"Now what is on that bright mind of yours?"

"Mrs. Rand," I started. "I'm worried about someone. You see, I have this good friend in my class at school. His name is Terry. He told me that his mother takes things."

"You mean she steals?" she asked, a bit surprised.

"Well, sort of. She doesn't really steal big or expensive things. Or rob banks or nothing like that. But she takes things from her jobs and brings them home. Terry's afraid of what will happen if

62

she gets caught. He's afraid she'll be arrested and sent to prison. Can someone be sent to prison for stealing things?"

"Well now, this friend of yours seems to be in a tough spot. I guess it depends on what his mother steals. A lot of people take little things home from their jobs now and then. If they work in an office, they sometimes take home a pencil or two, or a pad of writin' paper, or a box of paper clips. If they work in a bakery, they sometimes take home some cookies or cakes. I wouldn't call that real stealin'. It's the wrong thing to do, but no one ever went to prison for that, I don't suppose.

"My niece, Marion, out in California, is a school teacher. I remember her tellin' me once that at the end of every single day, she has what she calls pocket-shakin' time with her second graders. Those kids just seem to take whatever's layin' around. She told me it's just amazin' to see how many pencils and erasers get stuck into those little children's pockets. Why, one boy even took a jar of yellow paint from her closet and put it in his lunchbox.

"Although it's wrong, and grown-ups should know better than second graders, they don't think of takin' things like that as stealin'. They think of it as just bein' there, and the things are there to take."

"But what about a Mama—uh, Terry's mother—who takes bigger things than pencils, paper, or even a jar of paint and lots of them?" I asked.

"Well, I guess if she did get caught, she'd be fired right on the spot to teach the others a lesson. This boy's mother should know better. I'm sure she knows better. 'Thou shalt not steal' was written in the Bible a long, long time ago, and most people—grown-ups and children—accept that commandment. Besides it bein' wrong to do by law, stealin' is wrong to do for your bein'. No one should take anything that belongs to someone else. What does the boy's daddy say about all this?"

"His dad's dead," I said quickly. "And he has one—no, two little brothers."

"Oh, well, maybe they're poor. Too poor to buy things. Even though it's still wrong and even though 'Thou shalt *not* steal,' sometimes people earn so little money they feel the need to take things that don't belong to them. What kinds of things does the lady take?"

I had to think fast so Mrs. Rand wouldn't figure out it was Mama I was really asking about. I answered her, making believe Terry's mother worked in nearly the same kinds of places Mama worked in.

"Well," I said, "Terry told me that no matter where she works, she takes things. He told me she once worked in a clothing factory and took home all kinds of clothes for him and his little— his *two* little brothers," I quickly added. "She took socks, pants, shirts, ties, suit jackets, pajamas—even undershorts. Once she worked in a meat plant and took chickens and pork chops and lamb chops and hams and roast beefs and steaks almost every single day. Now she's working someplace else."

I had to think faster. I couldn't say a five-and-ten-cent store. That would surely give Mama away.

"She works in a . . . a hospital," I continued. "A hospital. And she takes home—uh—sheets. Lots of sheets and pillowcases."

"My, my, my," Mrs. Rand uttered. "Next thing you know, she'll be takin' home the patients! You say his daddy's dead? It seems to me that she has to work mighty hard to support herself and her children. Takin' things the way she does seems to say to me that she wants good things for her children. Raisin' boys isn't easy in these times, especially without a daddy to help. Maybe what this boy's mother needs is some understandin' and lots and lots of love. Maybe she thinks the kids really want or need these things to make them happy. Maybe she thinks that they love her for the things she brings home and not for herself. You know what I think? It might be her way of tellin' her love. I think this boy should talk to his mother. Tell her he's grown old enough now to know what she's doin'. And that he'd love her even more if they had to make good with what they've got.

"Lovin' sometimes creates a lot of problems, but it solves many of them, too. Lovin' has the power to change things. It can change this whole, wide, sometimes confusin' world. And in the end, lovin's better than stealin'. This woman *could* have a real bad problem, but it sounds more like this boy's mother is tryin' to tell her love.

"I have an idea. Why don't you talk to your Mama about your friend? Your Mama's in nearly the same boat as that boy's mother, bein' she doesn't have a husband either. And your Mama has two of you to bring up. Your Mama's a wonderful, wonderful person. She'll help you decide what to tell your friend."

"I don't want to talk to anybody else, Mrs. Rand. Not even Mama. You've told me enough. I'll talk to Terry at school tomorrow."

"*Sesame Street*'s over," my little brother announced, dashing into the kitchen with his empty milk glass. "Will you play Old Maids with me now?" he asked.

"Yes," I said, happy that my little brother came in when he did. "Let's go downstairs and play. Get your things together."

"Yippee!" he shouted, as he dashed back into the living room.

"Thank you, Mrs. Rand," I said. "You *are* a good listener. You're a good talker-to, too, Mrs. Rand. Mrs. Rand, can we keep our talk private? Like a secret? I don't want anyone else to know about Terry's mother—not even Mama."

"Cross my heart. Won't breathe a word. Some conversations

are meant to be kept secret and private. That's what brings friends like us together and keeps them friends forever."

"Ready?" my little brother asked, returning to the kitchen.

"Let's go," I said. "Thank you for watching my little brother— and for the milk and Christmas cookies. And the talk."

"No need to thank me at all. You tell your Mama I said hello, and tell her not to work so hard. She works far too hard and far too long, that woman. Far too hard and long."

"Bye," I said.

"I'm going to beat you," my little brother said. "You're going to be the Old Maid. I always beat you. I beat everybody."

He always does!

nine

"Mama saved the best surprise for last."

ONE OF THE WORST THINGS ABOUT CHRISTMAS was trying to decide what to get Mama. Since today was Christmas Eve, we only had a half-day at school. On my way home, I stopped in the drugstore and found the perfect gift for Mama. It was a round, blue powder box—and all plastic. On the lid there was a beautiful painting of two old-fashioned ladies dressed in long gowns, wearing high wigs, and holding fancy fans in front of their faces. When you lifted the lid, a tune tinkled. The plastic coating inside, where you keep the powder, just shined and shined under the drugstore's bright, fluorescent lights.

Mama's favorite color is blue, she always powders her face before she leaves the house, she likes music, the powder box wouldn't take too much room on her already crowded dresser, and it was all plastic. On the bottom of the box there was a label pasted on telling the name of the song—*Skater's Waltz*. I never heard of that song, but it sounded pretty to me, so I knew it would sound pretty to Mama, too. There was also a small sticker that said $3.98. I had saved up six dollars to buy presents for Mama and my little brother, so I had more than enough; this made the powder box even more perfect.

"I'd like this box," I said to the man behind the counter.

"Three-ninety-eight," he said. "That's including tax."

"It's for my Mama," I said, as he put it in a bag, "for Christmas."

"Good. Three-ninety-eight," he said.

I handed him a five-dollar bill.

He clanged the cash register and handed me two pennies and a one-dollar bill, saying, "Three-ninety-nine, four, five dollars. Thank you. I hope your old lady likes it."

I walked out of the store feeling mad at what the man had just said. I wanted to tell him that I *know* Mama will like it and that she's *not* an old lady. The nerve of him, I thought.

When I got home I went right upstairs to Mrs. Rand to get my little brother.

"Merry Christmas," said Mrs. Rand, opening the door.

"Hi!" I said. "Merry Christmas."

"You want some milk and cookies?"

"No, thank you, Mrs. Rand. I have to wrap up a present before Mama gets home. She's coming home early tonight. The five-and-ten-cent store closes at five o'clock today because it's Christmas Eve. My little brother and I are meeting Mama down at the bus stop."

"Well, I'll see all of you tomorrow, God willin'. It was so good of that Mama of yours to invite me to Christmas dinner again this year. She's a gem. Too many people think only of themselves at

Christmas and don't give much thought to the lonely. Your Mama's a wonderful person. Just too wonderful for words."

"Yes," I said, not knowing what else to say, as my little brother came to the door.

"Want to play Old Maids with me?" he asked.

"Not today," I answered. "It's Christmas Eve. We have to wrap Mama's present. Let's go. Bye, Mrs. Rand. See you tomorrow."

"You sure will. And Santa Claus just might be by my house tonight to leave some packages for both of you and for your Mama. He just might do that," she said, laughing gently.

"He might have something at our house for you, too, Mrs. Rand," I said, knowing Mama always got her a little Christmas present.

"By the way, how's your friend Tommy and his mother gettin' along?"

"Terry, not Tommy," I said. "He's fine. Everything will be O.K. I talked to him, and he's talking to Mama—I mean his mother—right after Christmas. Everything will be O.K. Bye, Mrs. Rand. Thanks for watching my little brother."

I wrapped Mama's present in tin foil and put a big red bow that I found in the box of Christmas stuff on the top of the package. I also made Mama a card and had my little brother print his name on it. I could hardly wait to give Mama her present. It's the best present I ever bought her. Even my little brother loved it, and he doesn't like anything but his deck of Old Maids.

At five-thirty, I helped bundle up my little brother, put on my coat, scarf, gloves, and boots, and went to the bus stop to meet Mama. We were both glad she was on the first bus because it was very cold outside. Mama came off the bus—her arms filled with bags.

"Santa Claus is here. It's Santa Claus time," she called.

"Where is he?" asked my little brother.

"Mama meant he's coming. Tonight," she said, giving me a wink.

"Mama, did you remember to bring home the thing I asked you to get. The O.M.'s for you-know-who?"

The O.M.'s was a new deck of Old Maids for my little brother. His old deck was nearly worn out from playing with it so much. I knew he'd love this for Christmas.

"I certainly did," Mama answered. "Mama never forgets anything. When I was a little girl, the teachers told your grandma, God rest her soul, especially on Christmas Eve, that I had a mind like an Einstein. 'A mind like an Einstein' is what they said about your Mama. He was a great scientist, you know."

"I know," I said. "I read about him at school."

"Like an Einstein," she repeated.

"What's that?" I asked, pointing to a large rectangular box Mama was clumsily carrying.

"A surprise. A nice surprise for the three of us. You'll see it later—tonight."

"What time are we going to George's to get the tree?" I asked.

"My, you're certainly busting at the seams with questions today. You ask too many questions. You know your Mama doesn't like questions. Only answers!"

Sometimes Mama makes me mad. What's wrong with a question like, "What time are we going to George's to get the tree?" I thought.

Once inside the house, Mama handed me the large rectangular box I asked about and told me to put it under her bed.

"There's no room under there," I told her. "It looks as if you cleaned out—I mean—*bought out*—the whole five-and-ten-cent store."

I turned as red as a beet from the slip of my tongue. I wanted to bite it off for saying that. I knew Mama caught that "cleaned out" because she winced and sternly said, "Then just put the box *on* the bed. *On* the bed. And get you and your little brother washed up for dinner. Now. Right now!"

After dinner I helped Mama dry the dishes. I wanted to ask again what time we were going to George's to get the tree, but I wouldn't dare. It was already seven, and George only stayed open until nine. I didn't want Mama to get mad at me, especially on Christmas Eve.

When the last dish was dried and put away, Mama said, "You go in the living room now and play Old Maids with your little brother. Mama has to do some Christmas surprising in her room."

"I don't feel like playing Old Maids," I answered.

"Then go watch TV till I call you. I'll only be a little while."

In the middle of the second batch of commercials, Mama called, "Come into Mama's room now. Both of you. Come in."

Mama stood at the open door and let us walk in.

"Wow! It's pretty," my little brother said, with his mouth and eyes open wide.

It was pretty. I never saw a prettier sight. Nowhere. Ever. Mama's bed looked like a tapestry—a Christmas tapestry. Silver-glowing icicles were stacked in boxes, box after box. Red and green ornaments, dozens and dozens of them, shone just like the star of Bethlehem must have shone. Lambs and cows and donkeys were all over the bedspread. Camels were everywhere. So were plastic candy canes. The three Wise Men turned out to be eighteen Wise Men: five carrying gold, six carrying myrrh, and seven carrying frankincense.

"Pretty, pretty, pretty," my little brother chanted, staring wildly at all the glitter and glow.

"Well?" Mama said. "Well? How do you like Mama's surprise. Isn't this a big Christmas surprise?"

"Yes, Mama. It's great," I said, casting my eyes on a stack of boxes of Christmas ball hangers and wondering how we would ever fit all this stuff on one Christmas tree.

"Now, I have the greatest and biggest surprise of all. Mama saved the best surprise for last."

She went into the closet, pulled out the large rectangular box, and opened the lid.

"Surprise! Surprise!" Mama shouted, holding up a big plastic tree. "I got us a tree. Your Mama said you'd have a beautiful tree this year, didn't she? I said it. I told you so the minute your little brother asked me. What Mama says she'll do, Mama does!"

No, I thought. No, no, no! Now I knew why Mama didn't answer me when I asked her about going to George's.

"It's fake, Mama," I said. "It's a fake tree. We always have a real tree."

"It's not fake," Mama said, proudly holding up the tree. "It's plastic. We can keep this tree from year to year. Look how nice it looks. Why, this tree looks even better than the real thing. Plastic keeps year to year, so now we won't have to go to George's anymore for his bargain trees which aren't bargains to begin with. No siree. No more of George's spindly real trees for this family! From now on, we'll have this fine, fine plastic tree to trim with all these lovely Christmas ornaments year after year. We won't have to go to George's for a tree anymore—never again. We won't have to pay him a dollar for a tree that's not even worth a dime tomorrow morning. The dollar we'll save will buy something else."

"A dollar's not much to pay for a tree, Mama. Not for a real tree," I said.

"A dollar is a dollar. Mama doesn't have a dollar to throw away on garbage—especially garbage trees."

"It doesn't smell like a real tree," my little brother said, looking as disappointed as I was.

"What difference does that make? You *look* at a Christmas tree. You don't go around *smelling* it. Only dogs go around smelling trees."

"It doesn't look like a real tree, either," I added, feeling just awful about the whole thing.

I looked at my little brother. He looked at me. We could both tell from looking at each other that we both felt the same way about the tree Mama was holding. Mama sensed something was wrong.

"What's the matter with the two of you? It doesn't *smell* real, it doesn't *look* real. It *is* real. It's plastic! Plastic is real, isn't it? It looks better than those spindly trees George sells, doesn't it? Look at the color. Look at the shape."

"We can get a real tree for only a dollar at George's tonight, Mama. It's less than what that tree must have cost. Plastic stuff usually costs more money than real things do."

"This tree didn't cost your Mama anything—not one cent. The store ordered way too many, and this was one of the leftovers. Leftover plastic stays fine forever, not like leftover real trees. This tree was free."

I couldn't begin to imagine how Mama got that big rectangular box out of the store. I knew she took it. I knew it. Just like she took all the Christmas things on her bed. The five-and-ten-cent store game was over for me, but Mama was still playing it — even on Christmas Eve.

"We saved one dollar of your Mama's hard-earned pay today. A dollar saved is like a dollar earned. Someone famous said something like that once."

The room became quiet. My little brother and I didn't say

another thing. I clenched my teeth tight together, squeezed my eyes shut tight to keep from crying, and ran out of Mama's room into mine. I opened my top dresser drawer and took out the cigar box that I saved my Christmas money in. I dumped it on top of the dresser and counted it. The dimes, nickels, and pennies added up to two dollars and two cents.

I counted out forty-nine cents and put it aside. That's how much I owed Mama for the deck of Old Maids she bought for me to give to my little brother. I scooped up the rest of the coins which came to a dollar and fifty-three cents, threw them in the cigar box, and went back into Mama's room.

"Here, Mama," I said, handing her the cigar box.

"What's this?" she asked.

"The change I've been saving. It's left over from my Christmas present money. There's $1.53 in there, Mama. It's enough to buy a real tree."

"Real tree, real tree, real tree," my little brother shouted. "I want a real tree, too, Mama."

I could have kissed him.

Mama sat down on the edge of the bed, opened up the box and began moving the coins around with her finger.

"Your Mama thought you'd both like a real tree— I mean a real, plastic tree," she said, sniffling.

"Don't cry, Mama," I said. "Please don't cry."

"Don't cry, Mama," my little brother said, too.

"Your Mama's not crying. Not at all," she said, crying. "Your Mama just thought you'd both like a better tree than we could afford, that's all. Your Mama only wants the both of you to have the best in life. You're Mama's whole life, her whole world. Mama only wants the best for you, that's all Mama wants. Only the best for her two boys."

Mama got up from the bed, walked over to her dresser for a Kleenex, wiped her eyes, blew her nose, turned around with a big smile, and asked, "What time is it?"

I looked at my watch.

"It's 8:15, Mama," I said.

"Well, 8:15 already, huh? You two boys had better bundle up quickly. George closes his store at nine tonight. We'd better get a move-on fast if we're going to get our tree. Come on now. Get your coats and boots on while Mama powders her face and puts on some lipstick. We've got to go and get our tree."

"Yippee!" my little brother shouted, running out of the bedroom.

"Thanks, Mama," I said, giving her a hug. "Thank you very much."

"Come on now, son. Get a move-on," she said, but clutched me so tight to her I couldn't!

Then, handing me the cigar box, she said, "You put your savings back. That's your money. Your Mama will buy the tree just as she always has and always will. We have to hurry now."

In a few minutes, Mama called, "Ready?"

"We're ready," I answered.

Mama was standing at the door with her coat on. Underneath her arm she was holding the plastic tree. As we went outside, Mama locked the door, put her keys in her purse, and walked over to the incinerator. She opened the incinerator door, pushed the tree in, and slammed the door closed. My little brother and I just looked at one another. We never saw Mama throw anything away— except for Great-aunt Bertha's prize-winning African violet!

"There!" Mama exclaimed. "It's all gone. No more fake trees in this house. Only real trees for my boys. My boys will only get what they want! Let's move on now. Button up. Mama doesn't want either of you to catch a cold. Not on Christmas Eve. Hurry now! Let's get to George's."

Ten

". . . we're a very special family. Very special."

THE TREES AT GEORGE'S WERE THE SAME picked-over-looking ones he had every year, but from the twelve that were left, we found a beautiful one.

When we got back home and took off our coats and boots, Mama said, "Let's all carry this stuff from Mama's bed into the living room and begin decorating. We'd better get started because we're going to have to make a few trips back and forth."

When we finished trimming the tree, you could hardly see any of the branches. Barely any green was visible. In fact, there were so many ornaments we couldn't fit them all on the tree. Boxes of things were left over. We probably had enough ornaments to trim the largest tree in the world. One thing for sure—we had enough boxes of Christmas ball hangers to trim *two* of the largest trees in the world.

Every single time Mama handed me a Christmas ball and hanger to put on the tree, a slight shiver went through me. If there was one thing I could live without forever it was the terrible thought that every single one of those tiny, steel ball hangers reminded me of my trips to the five-and-ten-cent store.

After we finished putting things around the bottom of the tree, my little brother asked Mama, "Why do we have three baby Jesus-us?"

He didn't ask about the long parade of Wise Men. He's too little, I guess, to know that there were only three instead of eighteen! I wasn't going to tell him.

"Everyone else has only one baby Jesus under their tree," Mama answered. "Only one. We have three baby Jesus-us because we're a very special family. Very special."

I love Mama very much, but I still felt awful about all those Christmas things—about Mama and me taking all that stuff from the five-and-ten-cent store—particularly baby Jesus-us! But I did feel good about the real tree and the three of us being together.

"Now that the tree's all dressed from top to bottom, Mama thinks it's time for both of you to get ready for bed. If Santa Claus comes by and sees you up, why, he'll just take his reindeer and fly away to someone else's house. That's what he'll do. Take his reindeer and fly away. We wouldn't want him to do that now, would we? Let your little brother wash up for bed first while you help Mama put some of this stuff away."

When my little brother went into the bathroom, Mama put her

arm around my shoulder and whispered, "Don't you ever tell your little brother that there isn't any Santa Claus, you hear? Never. I want him to go on believing until he doesn't anymore. Besides, there really is a Santa Claus. There really is. He's in your heart. He's in everybody's heart. No matter how old you get, you keep on believing in him, son. The same way we believe in each other."

"I will, Mama. Mama, thanks again for the tree. I'm glad you changed your mind. The real tree is beautiful, Mama. It's really Christmas now."

Mama came into our room to tuck us in. Before turning out the lights, she said, "Your Mama has something to tell the both of you. Something new and exciting. I quit the job at the five-and-ten-cent store. The work is too hard, and the hours are too long. I've been thinking of taking a new job that just opened up over at the little laundromat—the one right around the corner from George's Grocery Store. When I was there doing our laundry last week, Mr. Jacobs, the man who owns the place, told me the lady that works there now is leaving next week. I would only work nine-to-six from Tuesdays through Saturdays. And I'd have every Monday off because the laundromat is closed on Mondays. Why, I'd almost run the place by myself. I'd be just as important as the owner.

"Most of the customers bring their laundry in in the morning and leave. Your Mama would do their laundry during the day while they're at work, and they'd pick it up the next day. Besides the pay being good, Mr. Jacobs said that the person who takes the job can do her laundry for free. F-r-e-e. That'll save us at least a few dollars a week, and since I could walk to work, I would save all that bus fare going back and forth downtown. The laundromat is so close by that on Saturdays the both of you could come by and see me whenever you want to. It would be fun working so close to home. It would seem like we're not even away from one another. Not away from one another at all. I think I'll tell Mr. Jacobs to stop looking. I'm going to take that job. I'll call him the first thing the day after tomorrow."

"That sounds great, Mama," I said.

"Since I wouldn't start working at the laundromat until the day after New Year's Day, I'll have a whole week off starting now. Now that's some Christmas surprise, isn't it? We can have a whole week to do what we want. We can spend all that time together."

"Can we go and see the Christmas windows?" my little brother asked.

"We sure can, but I think the first thing I'm going to do is take you both to the museum, the big one uptown, where they make stuffed animals look so real they almost scare you. And we can go to Radio City Music Hall for the first time. We'll see a movie on a giant screen, and we'll see the biggest stage show you'll ever see in your whole life. They have dancing girls there called the Rockettes, and juggling acts, and a great big orchestra that comes right out from under the stage like magic. And we'll see the big, special Christmas show they have where actors and actresses make believe they're Bible people back in Bethlehem and come to see the baby Jesus born. They even bring in real camels for this show. Why it's a scene from right under our beautiful Christmas tree come to life. Like magic. Just like magic before your eyes. We'll have a wonderful week together. Isn't that a surprise? What a wonderful, wonderful Christmas this is!"

The week with Mama did sound great, but the laundromat job was the most exciting thing Mama told us about. There's not much she can take from a laundromat except maybe some soap powder or bleach!

I looked over at my little brother's bed to see if he was still awake. He wasn't. He was sound asleep. I'm glad that he's too young to know that what Mama did is terribly wrong. I wish I didn't know.

For most of the night, I lay awake trying hard in my mind to hear Mrs. Rand's words: *"Lovin' has the power to change things. It can change this whole, wide, sometimes confusin' world. And in the end, lovin's better than stealin'."*

As soon as I get the chance—as soon as Mama will let me—I'm still going to try to talk to her about taking things. If I do let her know I know, maybe she won't ever take another thing again. Ever! But until the time comes when I can talk to her, I'm going to tell Mama over and over again how much my little brother loves her; how very much I love her.

Christmas Day is a good time to begin. Starting tomorrow I'm going to give Mama all the love I can, all the love I have in me. No one could love Mama more than me. No one.